AF079323

ILLUSTRATED BY PAUL MORAN,
ADRIENN GRETA SCHÖNBERG
AND GERGELY FÓRIZS

WRITTEN BY BRYONY DAVIES
EDITED BY JOSEPHINE SOUTHON

COVER DESIGN BY ANGIE ALLISON
DESIGN BY ZOE BRADLEY

TAYLOR'S ON TOUR

Not content with performing to more than 50,000 fans every night in huge stadiums across the world, this pop megastar is also making time to see the sights, have fun and even make new music.

But sometimes even global superstars need a bit of time away from the spotlight, and Taylor is doing her best to blend in wherever she goes. Can you find her on each page, hidden in the crowds? She's not alone; you'll also need to find her three cats – Taylor couldn't possibly leave them behind! – plus her guitar, her sunglasses and her cool cowboy boots. There is also one special item to find in every scene.

You can find the answers, plus extra things to spot, at the back of the book.

BACK TO NASHVILLE

Taylor's made sure that her tour has brought her home to Nashville, USA, so she can revisit her country roots. There are cowboy boots and hats aplenty here, and the barn dances are in full swing.

Can you spot Taylor, her three cats and the other items below?

BUTTERFLY HOUSE

While transferring through Singapore Airport, Taylor has decided to visit the butterfly garden. It's full of fluttering butterflies, whose brightly coloured wings put even Taylor's costumes in the shade!

Can you spot Taylor, her three cats and the other items below?

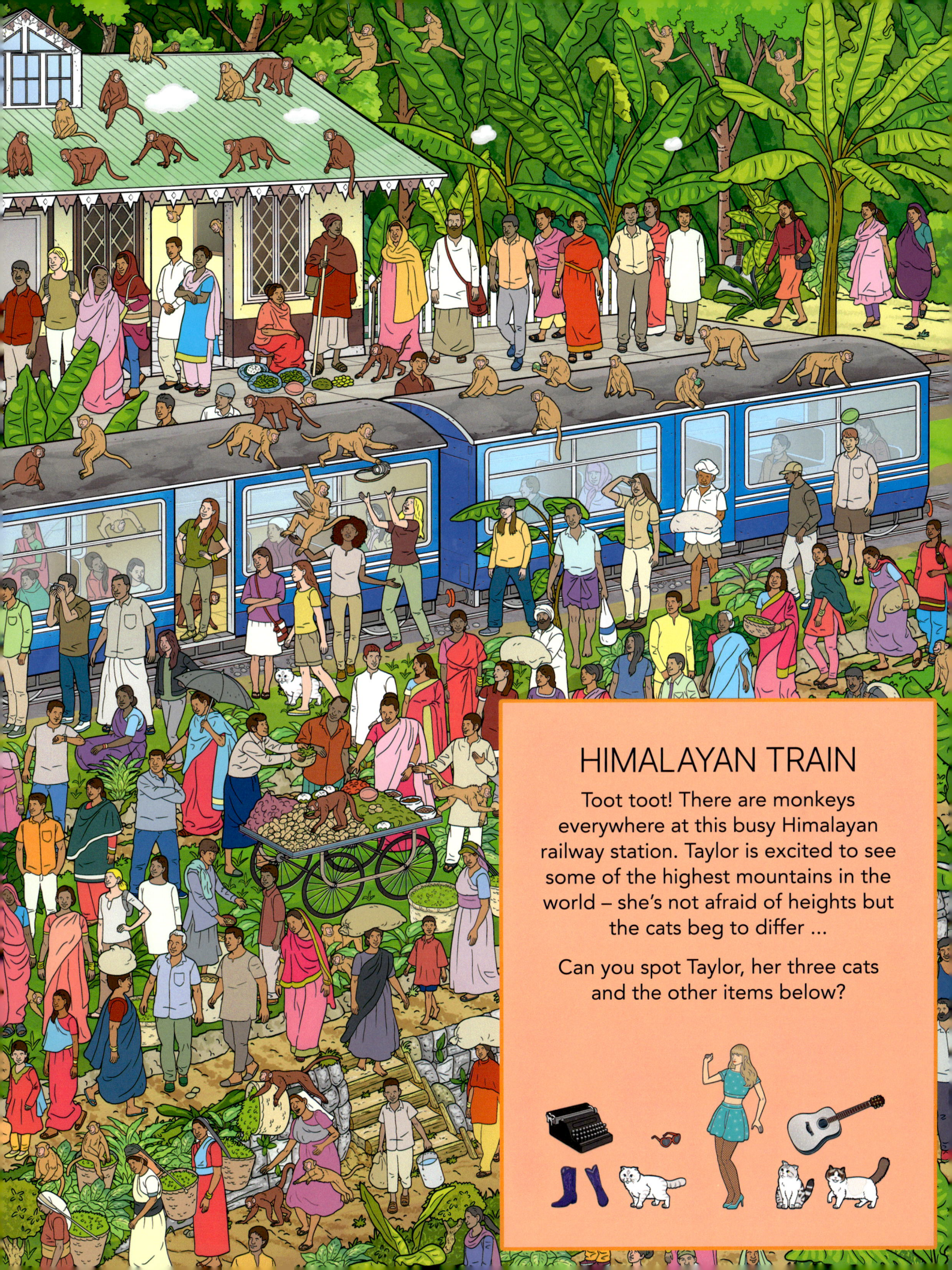

ANSWERS

SPOTTER'S CHECKLIST

- An exploding drink ☐
- Five owls ☐
- A broken guitar ☐
- A bird carrying a cowboy hat ☐
- Two lassos ☐
- Four raccoons ☐
- Nine foxes ☐
- A hot-dog stand ☐
- Three banjos (round guitars) ☐
- Four horses ☐

BACK TO NASHVILLE

BUTTERFLY HOUSE

SPOTTER'S CHECKLIST

- A leaping toad ☐
- Five water hoses ☐
- Two men wearing red jackets ☐
- Two people wearing yellow wings ☐
- Two girls wearing pink wings ☐
- Five green watering cans ☐
- Two women holding cameras ☐
- A woman wearing a red flowery dress ☐
- Two wheelbarrows ☐
- A girl wearing dungarees ☐

WELCOME TO NEW YORK

SPOTTER'S CHECKLIST

- A man riding a skateboard ☐
- A squirrel ☐
- A man taking a selfie with a hot dog ☐
- A dog diving into a pile of leaves ☐
- A breakdancer ☐
- A pigeon on a lamppost ☐
- Two ice hockey skaters ☐
- A woman having her portrait drawn ☐
- A man reading on a bench ☐
- Two people playing badminton ☐

MELBOURNE MARKET

SPOTTER'S CHECKLIST

- Three people wearing stilts ☐
- A tall hamburger ☐
- Three men wearing floral shirts ☐
- A fruit stall ☐
- A bird standing on someone's head ☐
- A woman dancing to guitar music ☐
- A bird stealing a man's doughnut ☐
- A green rucksack ☐
- One blonde woman holding a taco ☐
- A pink dress for sale ☐

MAGICAL VIDEO

SPOTTER'S CHECKLIST

- Seven black lanterns ☐
- A spinning wheel ☐
- A cuckoo clock ☐
- A green genie ☐
- A girl wearing one shoe ☐
- A hat with a yellow feather ☐
- A book with a rainbow on it ☐
- A donkey ☐
- A girl wearing a red cloak ☐
- A fox ☐

BEACH PARTY

SPOTTER'S CHECKLIST
- A surfboard with a panda on it
- Seven crabs
- A blue coolbox
- Someone falling off their surfboard
- A blue-and-white striped towel
- A man using binoculars
- Someone being buried in the sand
- A blue T-shirt with a shark on it
- A green inflatable dinosaur
- A bright-blue spade

ENCHANTED LIBRARY

SPOTTER'S CHECKLIST
- A goblin falling off a ladder
- A man with three grey hair 'horns'
- Twelve unicorn horn lamps
- A man with a monocle
- Two ladders
- A man with a golden unicorn head
- A long brown beard
- Two people wearing rainbow tights
- A woman holding a net
- An old man's golden walking stick

ICE-CREAM PARLOUR

SPOTTER'S CHECKLIST
- Five chalkboards
- Three ice-cream costumes
- A vending machine
- Five seagulls
- An ice-cream cone with five scoops
- Two mops
- A girl with pink hair
- A woman dropping a tray of food
- An ice-cream cone on someone's head
- A pink-and-white striped candy cane

HOT SPRINGS

SPOTTER'S CHECKLIST
- A board game ☐
- A puffin standing on someone's head ☐
- Four people wearing snorkel masks ☐
- An orange-and-yellow beach ball ☐
- Two water pistols ☐
- A yellow duck inflatable ring ☐
- A boy wearing a blue dressing gown ☐
- A group having their photo taken ☐
- Two boys wearing armbands ☐
- A woman reading a book ☐

SHANGHAI SENSATION

SPOTTER'S CHECKLIST
- Two dogs ☐
- A pink parasol ☐
- Three palm plants ☐
- A man holding a map ☐
- Five red parasols ☐
- A blue-and-pink tracksuit ☐
- A police vehicle ☐
- A sign with a panda on it ☐
- A red kite ☐
- A sign with a tomato on it ☐

HUSKY RACES

SPOTTER'S CHECKLIST
- Two ice hockey sticks ☐
- A snowman ☐
- A boy wearing a green coat ☐
- Three pink sleds ☐
- A man sitting on a rocking chair ☐
- A falling tree ☐
- Two rolled-up blankets ☐
- Someone skiing ☐
- A girl waving a yellow flag ☐
- Two wood-splitting axes ☐

HIMALAYAN TRAIN

SPOTTER'S CHECKLIST

- A teapot ☐
- Three bunches of bananas ☐
- A camera with a strap ☐
- A monkey stealing a hat ☐
- A grey parasol ☐
- Two monkeys eating apples ☐
- A bucket of water ☐
- Two white cows ☐
- A swinging monkey ☐
- Two upside-down monkeys ☐

SNOWY SCENES

SPOTTER'S CHECKLIST

- Two blue foxes ☐
- A reddish-brown scarf ☐
- Seven reindeer with golden-brown fur ☐
- A blue sled ☐
- A pair of flying reindeer ☐
- A child pointing to the sleigh ☐
- A blue crown ☐
- A pink-and-white bobble hat ☐
- A child wearing blue boots ☐
- A brown sack ☐

TRAFALGAR SQUARE

SPOTTER'S CHECKLIST

- Two horses ☐
- An accordion player ☐
- Two people on stilts ☐
- A red telephone box ☐
- Someone on a skateboard ☐
- A dog wearing sunglasses ☐
- A Union Jack flag ☐
- A tightrope walker ☐
- Two women taking a selfie ☐
- Someone juggling on a unicycle ☐

CUBAN BEATS

SPOTTER'S CHECKLIST

- A yellow laundry basket
- Three conga drums
- A white dog
- Four brown guitars
- A dancer in a bright-yellow dress
- Blue maracas
- Someone with pink shorts on his head
- Four floral shirts
- A blue rickshaw bike
- Someone serving churros

PET PARADISE

SPOTTER'S CHECKLIST

- Two fish tanks
- A paddling pool
- Three parrots
- A cat with an eye patch
- A bright-pink pet carrier
- A small group of sheep
- A brown cat in a pink bed
- A sausage dog in a shopping basket
- A bright-blue rucksack
- A dog kennel with a red roof

IN THE STADIUM

SPOTTER'S CHECKLIST

- A security guard wearing a feather boa
- Someone spilling a tray of drinks
- A large professional video camera
- Three cowboy hats onstage
- Someone getting caught in a dress
- A girl wearing a red hair bow
- Three people holding pom-poms
- A red-haired woman wearing a cape
- Four band members
- A woman wearing a blue, fluffy jacket

Manufacturer: First published in Great Britain in 2025 by Buster Books, an imprint of Michael O'Mara Books Limited, 9 Lion Yard, Tremadoc Road, London SW4 7NQ
www.mombooks.com

Represented by: Authorised Rep Compliance Ltd, Ground Floor, 71 Lower Baggot Street, Dublin D02 P593, Ireland
www.arccompliance.com

W www.mombooks.com/buster

f Buster Books

@buster_books

Copyright © Buster Books 2014, 2021, 2025
Copyright © Michael O'Mara Books Limited 2018, 2020, 2021, 2023, 2024

With additional material adapted from www.shutterstock.com

This book contains material previously published in *Where's One Direction?*, *Where's the Baby Unicorn?*, *Where's the Llama?*, *Where's the Panda?*, *Where's the Puppy?*, *Where's the Unicorn? An Epic Adventure* and *Where's the Unicorn in Wonderland?*

All rights reserved. You may not copy, store, distribute, transmit, reproduce or otherwise make available this publication (or any part of it) in any form, or by any means (electronic, digital, optical, mechanical, photocopying, recording, machine readable, text/data mining or otherwise), without the prior written permission of the publisher. Any person who does any unauthorized act in relation to this publication may be liable to criminal prosecution and civil claims for damages.

A CIP catalogue record for this book is available from the British Library.

ISBN: 978-1-83725-073-8

This book is not affiliated with or endorsed by Taylor Swift or any of her publishers or licenses.

5 7 9 10 8 6 4

This product is made of material from well-managed, FSC®-certified forests and other controlled sources. The manufacturing processes conform to the environmental regulations of the country of origin.

Printed and bound in October 2025 by Shenzhen Wing King Tong Paper Products Co. Ltd., Shenzhen, Guangdong, China.

For further information see www.mombooks.com/about/sustainability-climate-focus
Report any safety issues to product.safety@mombooks.com